THIS IS THE FIRS[...] WILL HOPEFULLY BE A SERIES OF BOOKS CHRONICLING THE ADVENTURES OF OSCAR AND AUSTIN. I HOPE YOU ENJOY IT!

JOSEPH HELSING

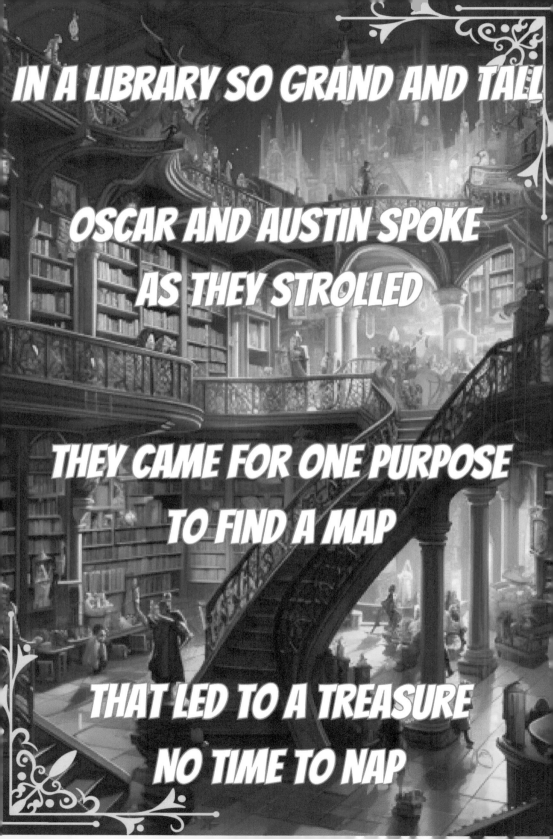

IN A LIBRARY SO GRAND AND TALL

OSCAR AND AUSTIN SPOKE
AS THEY STROLLED

THEY CAME FOR ONE PURPOSE
TO FIND A MAP

THAT LED TO A TREASURE
NO TIME TO NAP

THROUGH BOOKS OF ALL COLORS
SIZES, AND SHAPES
THEY LOOKED FOR THE MAP
THEY COULD NOT WAIT

IT'S SAID THAT IT LEADS
TO SPLENDOURLAND
A MYSTICAL PLACE
THAT IS SO GRAND

AND THEN THEY BOTH SAW IT
ON TOP OF A SHELF

THEY WOULD BOTH REACH FOR IT
THAT MAP LED TO WEALTH

OSCAR STARTED TO CLIMB
IT WAS A TALL SHELF

HE GRABBED IT IN NO TIME
SUDDENLY HE FELL

OSCAR TUMBLED AS
HE FELL DOWN

HE LOOKED FUNNY
JUST LIKE A CLOWN

AUSTIN LEAPT UP
AND CAUGHT HIS FRIEND

OSCAR WAS SO CLOSE
TO HIS END

OSCAR AND AUSTIN

SET OFF THAT NIGHT

ARMED WITH A LANTERN

THEIR SOURCE OF LIGHT

THE MAP SAID TO WANDER

UNTIL THEY SEE

A PORTAL SURROUNDED

BY FIFTY TREES

SOON THE BOYS WOULD FIND IT
IT LOOKED QUITE BIZARRE

IT GLOWED AND IT GLIMMERED
IT LOOKED LIKE A STAR

OSCAR HE STEPPED FORWARD
AUSTIN TOOK HIS HAND

SOON THEY WERE TRANSPORTED
TO ANOTHER LAND

THE SKY WAS SO PURPLE

THE TREES WERE SO BRIGHT

CREATURES RAN IN CIRCLES

THIS PLACE WAS A SIGHT

PAST THE WOODS A CASTLE

DIDN'T SEEM QUITE RIGHT

PERCHED UPON A DARK HILL

SURROUNDED BY NIGHT

AND THEN THEY BOTH SAW HIM
A BEAR IN A CAGE

THIS ALL LOOKED RATHER GRIM
OSCAR WAS ENRAGED

"WHO'S THE ONE WHO HURT YOU?
WHY HAVE YOU BEEN SHACKLED?"

"RUN! HE WILL HURT YOU TOO!
HE LIVES IN THE CASTLE!"

OSCAR ASKED:

"WHAT IS YOUR NAME?"

"FOZZLE," SAID THE BEAR IN CHAINS

"WE WILL RELEASE YOU," AUSTIN SAID

AS HE STROKED THE BEAR'S COLD HEAD

OSCAR FOUND A SCATTERED ROCK

HE USED IT TO BASH IN THE LOCK

THE BEAR WAS FREE
HE HUGGED THEM BOTH

AND THEN THE PAIR
THEY SWORE AN OATH

THEY SWORE THAT THEY
WOULD TAKE A CHANCE

THEY'D SAVE THE DAY
THEY'D MAKE A STAND

NO LONGER ZEROES
THEY WOULD STOP THIS PLOT

THEY WOULD BE HEROES
THIS VILLAIN WOULD ROT

THIS WONDERFUL PLACE
ONCE MAGIC AND GRAND

WOULD BE RESTORED WITH
THEIR HELPING HAND

OSCAR AND AUSTIN
THEY WOULD SAVE THE DAY

RAZZLE WISHED THEM LUCK

AS THEY WALKED AWAY

ALL THE PRISONERS
THEY WERE HELD BY MICE

CLAD IN BLACK ARMOR
THEY DID NOT LOOK NICE

AND THEY WERE ALL ARMED
WITH SWORDS AND WITH KNIVES

THE BOYS COULD BE HARMED
IF THEY RISK THEIR LIVES

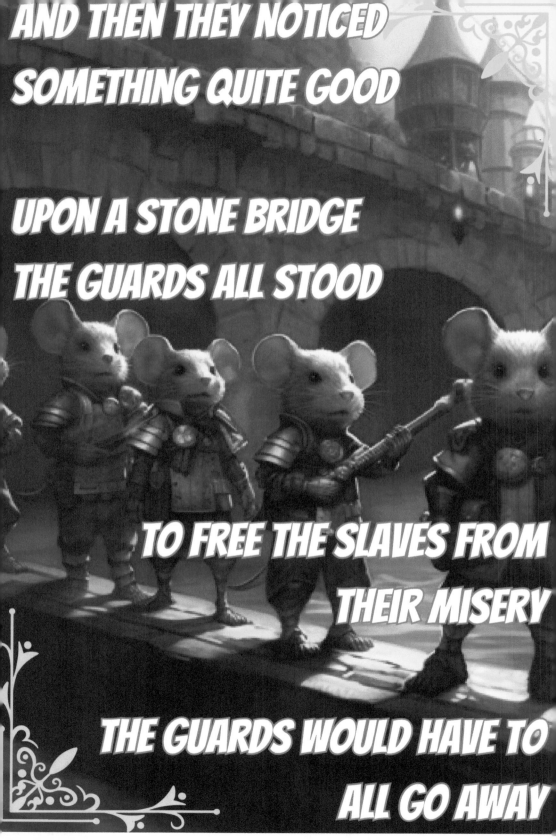

AND THEN THEY SAW IT
JUST OUT OF RANGE

A SWITCH FOR THE BRIDGE
BEHIND A CAGE

OSCAR RAN FOR IT
WHILE AUSTIN WATCHED

HE PRAYED THAT HIS FRIEND
WOULD NOT BE CAUGHT

OSCAR LEAPED UP AND
GRABBED THE SWITCH

BEFORE THEY KNEW IT
THE GUARDS ALL FELL

AUSTIN LAUGHED SO HARD
HE GOT A STITCH

HE WISHED THE GUARDS
GOOD LUCK IN HELL

THE FRIENDLY CREATURES
CHEERED AND CRIED

AS AUSTIN LED THEM
ALL OUTSIDE

THE HEROES JOURNEY'S
JUST BEGUN

THE CREATURES FREEDOM'S
NOT YET WON

WITH DYNAMITE
THEY FOUND INSIDE

AN EXPLOSION ROCKED
THAT HORRID MINE

WHAT WAS A PRISON
NOW WENT BOOM!

IT SPELLED AN END
TO ALL THAT GLOOM

THE CREATURES
NO LONGER OPPRESSED

THEY RAISED WEAPONS
AND EXPRESSED

THAT THEY MUST
SEE THIS STORY'S END

OSCAR AND AUSTIN
THEY'D DEFEND

THE PRISONERS
ALL STOOD WITH THEM

READY TO FIGHT
UNTIL THE END

TOGETHER THEY
WOULD STORM THE LAIR

AND END THIS LANDS
DARK DESPAIR

THEIR JOURNEY CONTINUED
A LITTLE LONGER

AS AN ARMY
THEY WERE STRONGER

THEY CUT DOWN MONSTERS
IN THEIR WAY

AS THEY FOUGHT THROUGH
NIGHT AND DAY

THEY TRAVELED LONG
AND WINDING ROADS

THEY MOVED THROUGH
CAVES DEEP DOWN BELOW

THEY SCALED MOUNTAINS
AND SAILED UNDER

THEY SAW SOME
WONDERFUL WONDERS

AND THEN THEY REACHED
THE CASTLE'S GATE

IN THE COURTYARD
LOTS OF MONSTERS

IT WAS THE TIME
TO FACE THEIR FATE

CROWLEY WAITED
FOR THEM YONDER

THE CREATURES TOLD
THE BOYS TO GO

"GO AND STOP CROWLEY
AND PLEASE KNOW

WE VALUE WHAT YOU
BOTH HAVE DONE

BUT THIS FIGHT
HAS JUST BEGUN"

OSCAR AND AUSTIN
SCALED THE GATES
THEN RAN SO FAST
THEY COULD NOT WAIT

THE MONSTERS TRIED
TO CLAW AT THEM

THEY DIDN'T STOP
UNTIL THE END

AN OPEN WINDOW
WAS THEIR GOAL

OSCAR LAUGHED
WITH SUCH DELIGHT

AS THEY LEAPED
INSIDE THAT HOLE

IT WAS TIME FOR
THE FINAL FIGHT

IT'S TIME FOR
THE FINAL BATTLE

RELEASE THIS LAND
FROM IT'S SHACKLES

OSCAR AND AUSTIN
SCALED THE STAIRS

THEY MUST BE BRAVE
AND BE PREPARED

WAITING FOR THEM
UP ON THE ROOF

WAS THE VILLAIN
THEY'D PURSUED

IT WAS TIME TO
FACE THE TRUTH

THERE WAS ONE THING
NOW TO DO

CROWLEY LAUGHED
WHEN HE SAW THEM

HIS EYES WERE GLOWING
LIKE A BEAST

HE TOLD THE CHILDREN
"IT'S YOUR END"

"I WON'T REST TILL
YOU'RE DECEASED"

CROWLEY FOUGHT WITH
ALL HIS MIGHT

BLOWING FIRE
CASTING SPELLS

OSCAR AND AUSTIN
RAN INSIDE

HOW WOULD THEY FIGHT?
THEY COULDN'T TELL

WITH DARK MAGIC
ALL AROUND

OSCAR AND AUSTIN
RAN DOWNSTAIRS

THEY COULD NOT
AFFORD TO BE FOUND

AUSTIN STARTED
TO SAY PRAYERS

THE BOYS WERE
RUNNING OUT OF TIME

HOW COULD THEY
FIGHT THIS EVIL MAN?

HAD THEY REALLY
BEEN SO BLIND

TO COME HERE
WITHOUT A PLAN

A MOMENT LATER
THEY WERE FOUND

CROWLEY CACKLED
WITH DELIGHT

HE THREW THE CHILDREN
ON THE GROUND

BUT SUDDENLY THERE
WAS A LIGHT

THE CASTLE DOORS
HAD SWUNG OPEN

AND STANDING THERE
OUR FURRY FRIENDS

THE BOYS, THEY
FELT SUCH EMOTION

KNOWING IT WAS
NOT THE END

CROWLEY WAS BLINDED
BY THE LIGHT

HE FIRED A SPELL
BUT ITS NOT RIGHT

THE SPELL SHOT
RIGHT BACK AT HIM

CROWLEY DISSOLVED
FOR ALL HIS SINS

THE BOYS AND CREATURES
THEN ERUPT

THE VILLAIN'S DEATH
WAS QUITE ABRUPT

AND THOUGH THE FIGHT
WAS NOT AS PLANNED

THEY HAD ALL JUST
SAVED THE LAND

WITH THINGS SET RIGHT
THEY HAD TO GO

OSCAR AND AUSTIN
LOVED THE SHOW

THEY SAID GOODBYE
TEARS IN THEIR EYES

BUT FOREVER
THEY'D BE ALLIES

BACK TO THE PORTAL
THEY MUST GO

WITH A HEAVY HEART
THEY STEPPED INSIDE

THEY WERE ENVELOPED
IN THE GLOW

AND THEN STEPPED
OUT THE OTHER SIDE

THE BOYS WERE
HEROES ON THIS DAY

THEY HELD HANDS AS
THEY WALKED AWAY

THEY WOULD BE
FRIENDS FOREVER

AND HAVE LOTS
OF ADVENTURES

Ingram Content Group UK Ltd.
Milton Keynes UK
UKHW052233050623
422930UK00004B/107